Ten Timid Ghosts on a Christmas Night

Ornaments

Christmas
Lights

For my mom and dad, Lee and Norman Barrett—
Remembering all of our Christmases together

Illustrations done in acrylic paints on paper.

SCHOLASTIC, CARTWHEEL BOOKS, and associated logos are trademarks and/or registered trademarks of Scholastic Inc. No part of this publication may be reproduced, or stored in a retrieval system, or transmitted in any form or by any means, electronic, mechanical, photocopying, recording, or otherwise, without written permission of the publisher. For information regarding permission, write to Scholastic Inc., Attention: Permissions Department, 557 Broadway, New York, NY 10012.

Library of Congress Cataloging-in-Publication Data
O'Connell, Jennifer Barrett.
    Ten timid ghosts on a Christmas night / by Jennifer O'Connell.
        p.   cm.
    Summary: Ten timid ghosts are visited by Santa Claus and learn what Christmas feels like.
    ISBN 0-439-39553-4
    [1. Christmas–Fiction. 2. Ghosts–Fiction. 3. Santa Claus–Fiction.
4. Counting. 5. Stories in rhyme] I. Title.
PZ8.3.O265 Te 2002
[E]–dc21   2002020980

10 9 8 7 6 5 4 3 2 1   02 03 04 05 06
            Printed in the U.S.A. 24 · First printing, October 2002

Ten Timid Ghosts
on a
Christmas
Night

by Jennifer O'Connell

SCHOLASTIC INC. Cartwheel B·O·O·K·S®

New York   Toronto   London   Auckland   Sydney
Mexico City   New Delhi   Hong Kong   Buenos Aires

1 One timid ghost on a Christmas night—
Waiting and watching by candlelight.
She heard a jingle in the dark outside
And rushed to the window—her eyes open wide.

2 Two timid ghosts on a Christmas night—
Waiting and watching by candlelight.
They looked outside and, up in the sky,
A team of reindeer was flying by.

3 Three timid ghosts on a Christmas night—
Waiting and watching by candlelight.
They heard a clatter and a "ho, ho, ho"
From up on the rooftop out in the snow.

4 Four timid ghosts on a Christmas night —
Waiting and watching by candlelight.
They saw a sleigh on the roof so high —
Shiny red in the snowy sky.

Five timid ghosts on a Christmas night—
Waiting and watching by candlelight.
They felt frosty air from the fireplace,
So they hid in the kitchen, just in case.

Six timid ghosts on a Christmas night —
Waiting and watching by candlelight.
They heard a *THUMP* in the living room
And peered down the hallway into the gloom.

7 Seven timid ghosts on a Christmas night—
Waiting and watching by candlelight.
They heard some rustling and a merry hum.
They crept in closer to see who had come.

Eight timid ghosts on a Christmas night —
Waiting and watching by candlelight.
They peeked round the corner
    and saw chocolates and fruits,
Peppermint candies...and big, black boots!

Nine timid ghosts on a Christmas night—
Waiting and watching by candlelight.
They spied ten stockings hung in a row
And someone in red by their tree all aglow!

Ten timid ghosts on a Christmas night—
Waiting and watching by candlelight.
They saw so many presents and, up at the top,
A bright, red hat going hippity-hop....

One startled Santa on a Christmas night
Gave ten timid ghosts a great big fright!

"Hello!" said Santa. "There's no need to fear.
I've come to bring you some Christmas cheer!"

The ghosts opened gifts
On that cold winter's night,
Laughing with Santa
By the Christmas tree light.

And when it was time for Santa to go,
Up the chimney he went, out into the snow.
The ghosts waved good-bye as his sleigh took flight.
"Merry Christmas to all on this wonderful night!"